Trouble On Top

Bromance Chronicles 1

Billie Bloom

Trouble On Top
Previously published as, The Rulebreaker
Copyright © 2021 Billie Bloom
All rights reserved

billiebloomromance.com

Edited/Proofed by K.C. Enders

Cover Design by Uplifting Author Services

Kendall, I finally did it, thanks to you.
You continue to be my hero after all these years.

Chapter 1

Grayson

THREE YEARS AGO

Well, there he is. I'm blatantly eye fucking my roommate's brother. It's shameless. But I can't help myself.

Coach Reiner has been drooling over Parker Miller, too, but for a very different reason. He needs to find my replacement since I'm graduating this year and Parker is the hottest recruit for goalie for the Michigan University Stags hockey team. Hell, he's the hottest recruit in the nation, for that matter. I'm sure scouts have already approached him about his pro career. Not that I'm jealous ...

Normally, guys attend our two-day tryout event, but not in this case. Coach Reiner has arranged a solo session just for Parker.

Parker is not great at being on time to things; I at least know that about him. So we're off to a solid start here. But he's so damn good, it doesn't matter.

Our center and wingers set up to stretch Parker out. As soon as the shootout starts, my envy fades, replaced by pure awe. Parker makes this look gymnastic. He's fast as lightning and accurate as a laser. Getting one clean catch after another. Making our senior players look bad for fuck's sake. Hashtag goals.

I've been living with Parker's brother, Cameron, for four years now, but I've never seen Parker play. That wouldn't be so weird, but their parents, Dale and Ellen Miller, unofficially adopted me when they learned I aged out of foster care and had nowhere to go during college breaks. You'd think I might have caught a game by now with how often I hang out with this family.

Dale and Ellen have also been helping me prepare for my career in professional sports, navigating the agent selection process. I wasn't sure I'd get picked up to tend goal, but at the very end of the season my senior year, I'm finally in talks with the Astor Agency. They're my dream group too. Based in New York, specializing in hockey, and snatching up all the goalies in the league.

When Parker finishes his tryout—with the bulk of the MU Stag team watching from the stands—the arena erupts in applause. Parker rips off his helmet and flashes his devilish smile that melts all the new waves of bitterness I feel.

I mean, he should be the one signing to an agency right now. I don't know why he wants to play for a college team. I guess it's a growing trend though, more and more NHL prospects are playing four years in college with full rides. Not that Parker needs a full ride, his parents are millionaires.

When Parker clears the ice, our team finishes out the last practice before our final game of the season. We didn't make the Frozen Four like we did last year, so our season is ending early.

I get in the net, and the team starts firing off shots at me. Inspired by Parker, I'm going harder than I have in a while. So hard in fact, that I hear a loud snap ricochet off the ice. Everyone freezes in place and looks at me. I look at my stick, it's not broken, so it wasn't that.

A second later I actually feel it, my groin is burning. Doubled over in pain, I can't even get off the ice.

The guys race over to me. Coach runs across the ice in his tennis shoes. Before I know it, the team trainer is there, then a medical crew. Soon I'm loaded onto a stretcher in full gear. Then I'm sweating it out in the back of an ambulance, rolled into a hospital, cut and stripped, x-rayed and diagnosed. Hours go by and they say two words that no goalie ever wants to hear: *Athletic pubalgia.*

***

Even after a month of rest and recovery, I'm still feeling awful. The doctors call it inguinal disruption and it's most likely a career ender.

The Astor Agency has effectively shredded my contract.

My life is officially over.

I'm lying in bed in my apartment in agony. I've pushed my boyfriend Cal to his limit in his role as caregiver. He's starting to hate me. Maybe if Cameron hadn't moved home early this year things would be better. I should have gone with him, and taken the Miller's up on their offer to let me recover at their house. Damn my guilt. But, shit, I might have to call them.

I wake up late, after a nap, to the sounds of a loud porno playing in the living room. Cal's distinctive moans are a part of the mix, though. *What the fuck?* I really shouldn't stand up, but I do anyway because my stomach is sinking in fear. I shuffle myself to the living room as I cringe in pain.

Cal is buck naked with some guy leaned over the couch.

"What the fuck!" I roar at him. He doesn't even try to stop. The guy he's with jumps though, reading the room like a proper human, scooping up his clothes and running out the door.

"Get out Cal. Just get the fuck out!" The bastard has the nerve to smile at me as he slowly dresses. He must really hate me. When he closes the door behind him, I slink to the bed. Tears spill out of my eyes. I dial up Ellen Miller. In less than an hour, she and Dale are here to bring me home.

Cameron and Dale have to practically carry me up the stairs. They settle me into my usual guest room. My eyes are red and puffy from the tears. I just don't think life can get any worse right now. But of course I'm wrong about that too. Parker Miller is watching me from the doorway of his room with wide eyes, looking young and free and on top of the world. Everything I'm not. Fuck. My. Life.

Chapter 2

Parker

It's no wonder my parents are throwing a blowout party. There's a lot to celebrate. My older brother Cameron was accepted into law school at Michigan University. I just got a full ride to MU for hockey. Everything's coming up Miller lately.

There are literally hundreds of people wandering our property, swimming in the pool, zipping around on the jet skis, jumping on the oversized trampoline, playing beach volleyball, gorging on food. It's a combination of Cameron's friends and my friends and my parents' friends. It's madness.

I'm bouncing around from group to group because as Mom says, I'm a social butterfly. That, and I have ADHD, so I'm distracted easily by shiny things, much like a fish.

I'm also a huge flirt and there are a lot of sexy people here, girls and guys alike. The latter is a little new for me, finding guys sexy I mean. Sure, my bunkmate and I gave each other summertime handies at hockey camp, but I honestly thought we were just helping each other out.

It turns out that's not something all guys do. I know because I asked my best friends, Chase Henry and Johnny Xu, about it. After a good amount of ribbing me for my ignorance, I learned that apparently, they hadn't been jerking off their roommates at hockey camp. I definitely encouraged them to try, though. Guys give the best handies.

Speaking of guys who I want to touch my dick, Grayson Price is sitting alone looking out at the water.

Since I first looked at guys, I noticed him, but I was just some high school kid all these years. Until now that is.

I wasn't supposed to know that he's gay, but I do. Actually, I'm one of the few who do. I've stayed with Cameron and Grayson enough to be let in on that secret. Why it's a secret, I don't totally get. I guess Gray didn't want it to affect him in the NHL. With his injury, though, that's out the window now, right?

I stroll up to him and slide into an empty chair.

"What's wrong?" I ask, taking note of his scowl.

He grunts in reply.

Nonverbal, I see. That's fair. He's been so quiet since he got here. I would be too, if I just lost my pro career in a groin-busting save during a practice, no less. I swear when I saw it, my groin hurt for him.

If he's not going to say anything, I'm happy to do the hard work for him. I hold out my forearm. "Got the Stag logo tattooed on me last week. Mom flipped her shit."

He glances at it briefly. "Good line work."

I reach over and brush my finger across the Stag tattoo on his arm. "Still looks good." My voice cracks unexpectedly.

A zing of heat rushes through me when I touch him. I want Grayson, bad. I want to do a host of things with him that I've never tried before.

It's been torture having him down the hall from me. I've wanted to sneak down to his room so many times, but he's seemed so hurt and sad these past few weeks. I need to find a reason to get him alone. Maybe, then, I can work on cheering him up.

"You want to see something?" I rise up to my feet.

He gives me a skeptical look, one dark eyebrow lifting. "Does it involve me walking?"

"Yes. But I can be your leaning post. I've got you, big guy." I can't temper my flirting around him.

He frowns at me. "Does it get me out of this party and back to my room at the end?"

"I can make that happen." I wag my eyebrows.

"Fine." His scowl is still unchanged, but I'm thrilled anyway. Grayson, alone with me. Yes please!

I pull him up from the chair and he wraps his arm around my shoulder. He's bulky and warm and hard as a rock. His touch feels incredible. I want to touch him in so many more ways.

I bring him up to my room, which is very close to his room, so I'm making good on my bargain. I sit him on my bed and close the door. He actually blushes. I like it. His frown has softened, just a little.

He leans back on my headboard. "Uh, should I be in here with you?"

I laugh. "You say that like we're doing something wrong."

I swear he pinkens more and I like it. I suddenly feel the wrongness he was talking about though. Like there is heat between us. It's definitely not just me. It surprises me because I'm not used to having chemistry with a guy. Hand jobs with my hockey camp bunkmate made me horny, but I didn't feel that tingle in my chest like I do around Grayson. I'm jittery and nervous.

I bite my lip and drink him in, shamelessly adjusting my swelling cock while he watches.

He clears his throat and looks away. "You wanted to show me something?"

Oh, I'll show you something all right.

"Right. Shit. Sorry. ADHD. Check this out." I bring his attention to the puck displayed on my bookcase.

"Is that ..." he starts his question as he stands up from my bed and shuffles over to me.

"Yup. A Patrick Roy autographed puck." I beam proudly. "Dad got it for me for graduation."

He shakes his head, gazing down at the puck in wonder. "Lord. Your parents are the best."

"They are." I take a step closer to him as he leans in to examine the puck.

"You can hold it," I whisper into his neck.

Grayson is gorgeous. He has an angled jaw and high cheekbones and dark almond-shaped eyes. And his mouth is ... nope, not going to let myself think about his mouth—or all the wicked things I'd like to do to it.

"That's sacrilege." He shakes his head.

"Come on. Break the rules with me," I beg.

His eyes flash at me. I lick my lips at that moment. I want to break lots of unspoken rules right now.

I dare to invade his personal space. I step right between his legs so that we're pressed together from our chests to our thighs. I want him to feel how hard he's making me.

"We can't." His voice is stern. He steps away from me and hobbles back to my bed. He sits down and massages his groin.

"It still hurts?" I ask.

He sighs. "Yeah. I shouldn't have gotten up so soon after surgery."

"Why did you?"

He squishes his nose. "Long story. Ex-boyfriend drama."

"Right. Sorry." I do remember his frantic call to my mom. I didn't mean to overhear it. She answered it on speaker while we were driving in the car. He was trying to hold it all together, but I could hear the wobble in his voice, the tightness in his chest. Mom insisted he come stay here and recover.

I join him on my bed. I can't believe that Grayson Price is in my bedroom. Dirty thoughts are clouding my brain. I inch my way closer to him. He smells faintly like cocoa butter. I breathe him in.

"Mmhmm." I shift up next to him.

"Parker …" His voice is a warning but I ignore it. He stands up and I rise to meet him, grabbing him from behind, pressing my body against his.

I feel him melt against me. Dirty ideas flash in my mind. I want his clothes on my floor and his dick in my mouth.

Fuck it. I'm going for it. I trace my tongue across his neck. I want to spin him around and take his lips, but I hold back. I let my hands trail down his flat stomach, landing on his cock. He's as hard as I am. I move my fingers to untie his swim trunks.

He clasps his hand over mine to stop me and my heart sinks.

"Please," I groan into his ear. "I want you."

Grayson turns around to face me. "You're too young."

"I'm an adult."

"You're not gay."

"I'm gay enough to know I want to suck your dick," I eloquently argue.

"You're trouble." He scorns me.

"Couldn't agree with you more," I tease.

"I'm on the rebound."

"I know how to tie up and pounce on the rebound."

He smiles at my goalie reference. I knew I could get him.

He stares at me for a long time.

I make puppy dog eyes. "It's just a blow job between two consenting adults. Please don't turn me down. It's my graduation party and you didn't get me a present."

"You're relentless."

"True. And I always get what I want."

He scoffs as if agreeing.

I step closer, bringing my lips just inches from his.

"I'm going to kiss you now," I announce.

He doesn't protest. I may have been fapped off by a guy before, but I haven't kissed one. Or sucked dick. I want to, though. I *really* do. Especially with Grayson. I wet my lips and lean into him.

Chapter 3

Grayson

I should so not be kissing my best friend's eighteen-year-old brother in his bedroom. I need to stop this. Just one more minute. Okay maybe two. Finally, my sense returns and I wrench myself away from the warm sweetness of Parker's lips.

"'M sorry," I mutter and hobble back.

He looks at me with wet swollen lips, chest heaving. Fuck, he's sexy.

I have to turn around right here and now or I'll be making a mistake I can't correct.

I wander back down to the party and resume sulking on the beach. Even if I wanted to tackle Parker's innocent ass down on his bed and fuck him, I can't. My groin is too weak. How depressing is that?

Plus, he kind of annoys me. He's all bright eyed and bubbly with four years to look forward to at MU as my replacement.

I hate to admit it, but he's heaps better than I ever was, even as an incoming freshman. As long as he doesn't get injured, he's guaranteed to go pro. Envy pangs in my chest.

The final reason I can't fuck him … he's my best friend's little brother. His parents are the ones currently housing and feeding me. It would be the exact wrong way to repay everyone's kindness.

When the party wears down and the guests leave, Dale and Ellen Miller serve us up night caps in the big living room. They even let Parker have a drink because they're those kind of parents. Cameron has had several too many, so he sips on some water—sunburnt and slumped in a chair.

"I'm bisexual," Parker announces to the quiet room and I choke on my drink.

His parents' eyes go wide as they look at each other for a second before returning to normal.

"That's nice, dear." Ellen smiles and pats Parker's leg.

"Good for you, Son," Dale adds.

"That's all?" Parker asks tentatively.

"Are we supposed to make a bigger fuss?" Ellen asks as her brows knit together.

"Guess not." Parker shrugs. Everything in life is so easy for him. Even coming out.

"How's the leg?" Dale turns to ask me.

I purse my lips into a frown. "Terrible." I shift to get more comfortable.

"You know you're welcome to stay here when your lease ends," Ellen says sweetly.

I shake my head. "The Astor Agency offered me a job since they can't sign me to a team."

Dale claps his hands. "That's great news!"

"Congratulations," Ellen chimes. "So where are you going then? Do you need us to help move you?"

They're so kind to me. "It's in New York, but they gave me a moving allowance."

"We'll still come help you set up," Ellen concludes. Once the Millers are set on something, there's no changing their minds.

I'm grateful for all their support, even if I feel like I should keep a mental tally of all the nice things they've done for me so I can repay them someday.

"Better walk this one to bed, Park." Dale points to Cameron who's slumped over, leaning half off the chair.

Parker scoops up his brother. Cameron is a lot smaller than him, though just as tall.

"I think I'll head up too," I announce and follow them upstairs.

Once I settle under the covers in the guest room, I stare up at the ceiling. There's a soft knock at the door.

"Yeah?" I ask.

The door cracks open and Parker steps through. "Mom wants me to check to see if you need any more ice before bed?"

"I'm okay."

Parker holds out the ice bag in his hand. "She actually made me bring it up."

We both chuckle at that.

"Okay then." I wave him over and throw my blanket down as I take the ice pack and place it in the crook of my groin.

Parker closes the door and sits down on the bed. *What is with him and trapping us together in bedrooms?*

"So New York, huh?" he asks.

I nod.

"That's a shame." He sighs.

"Why? You'll miss me?" I'm only joking when I say it, but to my surprise he answers, "Yeah." I always forget that this family is not shy with their feelings.

"I'll be back for holidays and I'll catch some of your games," I smile weakly.

Even though Parker is hot, and after that kiss today I'm thinking all sorts of new thoughts about him, it's hard not to hate him just a little bit. He has a future. The future I wanted. I don't even know what my future is now. A month ago, I had a boyfriend who was ready to travel the country with me as I started a pro hockey career. Now I'm single and moving to a big city I've never even visited, to start a career I never wanted.

Parker changes the subject. "So I came out earlier."

I laugh at that. "Big reveal." I wave my fingers dramatically.

"I was serious though. I like guys. I'm nervous about going to college now. Like, I am experienced with girls but I won't know what I'm doing with guys."

I eye him suspiciously. We've never spoken like this before.

"You should be more nervous about being out. I was told by the scouts early on to keep my sexuality under wraps. It's hard to get picked up as a gay player. Certain sponsors won't want you, certain donors …" I warn him. I don't mean to bring him down. But he needs to know.

He just shrugs though. "Fuck 'em then. I'm going to be me and that's that."

My eyes open wide in judgment and I frown. I don't argue though. My jealousy is rearing its ugly head again. Parker will get to be out in college.

I couldn't be. It drove my ex crazy. I think he only hung on because he thought I was going to be a wealthy celebrity when I started my NHL career. And then as soon as he had to take care of me after surgery and knew my career was likely over, everything changed.

"So, can you help me?" he asks, voice dropping low.

"With what?" I search his eyes, my heart hammering uncomfortably fast inside my chest.

"Getting some experience. I need to know how to give a good blow job."

My mouth drops open. "The fuck? No. Absolutely not. That's wrong on so many levels."

His face sinks.

I almost never see him with this expression. I hate that it's me causing it.

I start again. "We're like family. Your parents are like my parents. It would be weird down the road. Plus, you're too young for me." *And I hate you a little bit for having everything I want.*

"I promise I won't make it weird. And by the way, I'm eighteen now. Full grown adult. If we were, say, twenty-four and twenty-eight, the age difference wouldn't even matter. Please say yes." His tone is begging and commanding at the same time.

My dick perks up in interest. Why does he have to be so fuckable?

"It's a bad idea." I know I should shut this down, but I'm quickly losing the blood from my brain that I need for thinking.

He scoots closer to me.

"A really bad idea …" I add half-heartedly.

"That kiss though. You felt it too," he purrs at me.

He isn't wrong. I did feel it. I haven't felt that sort of electricity in a kiss since I can't remember when.

"I'm moving in a week …" I point out.

"It's just a one-time thing. I promise. We'll never mention it again." He runs his finger down my stomach and flicks the waistband of my boxers up, so they snap back down against my skin. I suck in a breath of air because he's just taken the wind out of me. Am I really going to let this happen? Shit. I totally am.

Chapter 4

Parker

I'm ninety percent sure that Gray is going to turn me down for the second time today. But that doesn't mean I'm not going to try. In fact, I think I see his resolve faltering. He takes the ice pack out from under the covers and tosses it to the end of the bed.

I slowly pull down the blanket covering him and damn if I'm not right.

He's hard. Fully tenting his black boxers, straining the slit in the fabric just enough that I can see a little peak of his dick. *Fucking hell.*

My chub inflates to full mast at the sight of him and I bite hard on my lip.

"One time," he rasps.

My brain takes a second to catch up and process the words. Holy fuck, he said yes.

He puts his hands behind his head. "Take me out." He nods at me.

My stomach jumps at his deep, commanding voice. Okay, I think I love being told what to do.

I pull down his boxers and his cock smacks the fabric of his t-shirt. I pull up his shirt to reveal his rock-hard abs. Holy hell.

"Stroke me. Use your spit."

I lick my palm and wrap my fist around the middle of his shaft. He's about the same size as me, maybe a little thicker. I start to slowly pump him, rotating my wrist just a little, the way I like it.

"Lick the tip." He nods his head at me like it's a challenge but, fuck, he's wrong because I so already wanted to do that.

I lean down and obey, flicking my tongue across the sensitive slick skin. A moan escapes my lips.

"That's right," he hisses. "Wrap your mouth around the tip."

I do as he says and feel a low, vibrating rumble in his chest.

"Fuck."

I grin.

"Give me suction."

I take him in my mouth and suck, steadying my breath through my nose to calm myself because I might come in my pants just from sucking on him.

Another deep groan pours out of him.

"Now flick your tongue around while you suck."

His words make perfect sense. I've never had a blow job like this, but I imagine it would be fucking fantastic.

As I drag my velvety tongue over his smooth skin, he groans encouragement. "That's it, Parker."

Damn, hearing my name on his lips, swirled with pleasure, is making an intense heat shoot through me.

Grayson stays really still, and I don't know how he does it. When someone sucks my dick, I thrust into their mouths. Then it occurs to me—his groin. He couldn't thrust if he wanted to.

"Take more," he growls.

I stop the sucking action and glide down his length as far as I dare. My tongue instinctively licks along the thick dorsal vein. I reach my hand up and gently stroke my fingers over his thighs, working my way to his sensitive sack.

He makes a helpless sound that I freaking love.

My dick throbs between my legs. It wants attention, but both my hands are busy.

As if reading my mind, Gray stops me. "Come up here." He beckons me with one finger.

I stand up and walk to the head of the bed. Without moving anything but his arms, he reaches over and shimmies down my sweats.

"Not bad." He smiles at the sight of me.

"Not bad?" I feign offense, grabbing my dick in my hand and stroking it once.

He watches me with a hooded gaze.

"Come closer," he orders as he licks his lips. I hold myself up to him as he takes me in his mouth. It feels sudden, even though I watched the whole thing unfold.

It's not like I've never had a blow job before, but something in me stirs because it's a guy. Not just a guy. It's Grayson.

I couldn't have told you four years ago when I first met him at Thanksgiving that I would want to hook up with him. I knew he was hot, but I didn't know what that meant yet. Now I'm sure.

After a few expert sucks that far exceed anything I've ever felt, I have to pull away from him before I go off like a rocket. I've learned enough from being with girls that you need to ask before you come in their mouth or they freak out.

"This okay?" he asks.

"Too okay." My voice is gravel. He gets my meaning and chuckles softly.

"Good. Have you ever frotted?" He raises an eyebrow at me.

My lip curls up on the sides in a mischievous smile.

"I've studied it," I admit, and we laugh together. "I want to try." I nod.

"Take your pants off and climb over me."

Grayson tugs his sweats down to his thighs, although he winces at the motion.

I hook my leg over him and crawl onto the bed. I shift so I'm seated in a straddle across him. As our skin makes contact and I feel his heat on me, I let out a moan. "This is incredible."

He chuckles again. "We're not even doing anything yet."

"Just touching you …" I trail off because I don't want to admit the rest. *Is amazing. Is life changing. Is addicting. Is everything I always wanted.*

I shift up, careful of his injury, and align our cocks.

"You studied you said, so it's time for your exam." His tone is steady, but the way he's breathing tells me he's just as excited as I am about this.

I grab us up together and start to stroke. We're both still a little wet from each other's mouths. The feeling of my dick pressed against him is a hundred times better than the electricity I felt just having my bare thighs on his. With my hand spread wide to grasp us both, it's not easy to be creative with my strokes. I can't work my wrist around in a little half rotation like I usually do. Instead, I manage just barely to keep a hold of us and tug ever so slightly.

I take in the heat in his eyes, the way his mouth has fallen open, his heaving chest, his tight abs, our cocks rubbing together. I savor every little pant and moan that escapes his lips. We're both trying to stay quiet even though this house is so big no one will hear us.

Grayson curses under his breath and lifts one hand to touch my jaw. My mouth finds his again.

His kisses are hot and frantic with just the right amount of tongue. He nods at me and I know what that nod means.

"Me too," I say on a shaky exhale.

His eyes snap shut, his body tenses and I feel his hot flow steadily dripping over my crown and fist.

I slow us down and enjoy the new moist friction as I let myself slip over the edge with him. I grunt and rocket uneven spurts that mark his abs. I can see that does something to him the way his eyes darken.

He drags a finger through the mess I've made on him with a sated smile.

Chapter 5

Parker

PRESENT DAY

Cameron graduated law school and passed the bar, but he insisted we not throw a party. So, of course, my parents rented out an entire restaurant and invited a hundred people. To them, that wasn't a real party.

My stomach flips when I catch sight of Grayson Price from across the room. Since Grayson left for

New York three years ago I almost never see him anymore.

That one night we spent together was only that—one night, just like I promised him it would be. Part of me still couldn't believe he'd gone through with it. I'm sure he had a bunch of good reasons why us hooking up would be a bad idea—and maybe it was, but that night was magic.

I've revisited our encounter many, many times in my fantasies over the years.

And now that he's here—in person? I can't resist. I make a beeline for him as if drawn by a string.

He's just as tall and delicious as I remember. His hair is a little shorter and he dresses better.

I grin. New York must have gotten to him.

Just before I can reach him, my parents envelop him and pepper him with questions. He answers their rapid-fire stream like a champ. Yes, being an agent is going well. No, he's not still dating that guy my mom warned him about. He's staying at the Weber hotel and it's fine there. Yes, he's eating enough.

He does look trimmer than I remember. I guess when you're not playing hockey some of that bulk will retract. Even in a polo and well-tailored jeans though, I can tell he's still got plenty of muscle.

Seeing Grayson, hearing his deep voice, our eyes meeting ... it all has me stunned, if I'm being honest. He was the first guy I really crushed on back when I was discovering why I liked to jerk off guys. And damn, remembering the way his voice rasped as he taught me to blow him still gets me off.

I had wanted to go all the way with him, but we came and then he asked me to let him get some rest. Also, I was really scared to try anal.

Anyway, I learned as a freshman in college that anal was awesome. I like to top, I like to bottom. I like to top while I bottom and bottom while I top. So many fun ways to play when it's boys and girls and more than one person.

Unfortunately, the fun stopped a half a year ago when a scout informed me that I had an "undesirable reputation" and that coupled with the "gay thing", I might be unsignable due to questionable "morality".

So yeah, I got my act together and managed to keep it in my pants for a record six months now.

If a light breeze blows, though, I might explode. My dick is begging me to give up my hard-fought chastity now that Grayson fucking Price is standing in front of me, smelling amazing—like cocoa butter.

Finally, my parents have their fill of twenty questions and get distracted by another party goer. When they peel away, I'm left standing face to face with Grayson.

My pulse quickens and my hands start to sweat. I'm usually smooth but I have no idea what to say to him. Apparently, he doesn't either, because he's not saying anything.

This is a long time to stare silently at someone, right? I think so.

"Hi," I manage.

"Hey," he replies.

Okay. So that's out of the way. Now what? *Want to come back to my apartment?* No, too forward. Let's stock that question away for later.

"How's New York?" I ask. That sounded natural. *Nice work, Parker.*

"I've gotten used to it. How's hockey?"

I pout. "You haven't been watching my games?"

He laughs at that. "I have."

"So why'd you ask!" I scold him.

"I wasn't sure what to say to you," he admits. He's braver than me. I would never admit that.

"Nervous because I'm so devastatingly handsome?" I wag my eyebrows at him.

"You haven't changed much." He laughs again.

"I've changed in all the ways that count," I assure him in a more serious tone.

"I should tell you something up front." Grayson frowns. His words scare me.

I wait for him to continue, trying to not let my face fall too much.

He takes a deep breath. The suspense is killing me.

"The Astor Agency asked me to scout you this season. I wasn't able to come up with a reason to say no. I tried telling them we're like family, but I think they liked that. I didn't know if I should tell them about our past. I mean, I guess I should. I can do that, and they'll reassign you to someone else. I wanted to check with you to see if it was necessary. I mean, if you're not even considering them, maybe we don't need to disclose it."

"Astor?" My face lights up.

Grayson nods.

"And they want you to be my agent?"

"We work in teams, but yes, I'd be the acting agent."

"Don't tell them," I say conclusively.

His frown deepens.

"No, I mean, I definitely will consider Astor seriously, but if I do, I'd only consider them if you'll be my agent."

"That's a bad idea Park." Grayson shakes his head. Why does he look so good when he frowns? One simple conversation, and I'm practically vibrating with desire for him.

"It's a great idea." I beam. Having an excuse to spend more time with Grayson is totally worth keeping this secret. I want to be around him. I'm not about to give that up.

His face is mixed, but I can tell he's considering it.

"Look. I like Astor, but I'd like it more if I felt like someone I can trust is on the inside. Let's just at least talk about it more. Don't you have an expense account to wine and dine me? Let's do that. Take me to dinner and let's talk about it more. We don't have to decide anything yet," I proposition.

Finally, a smirk returns to his face, even if only tentatively. "Fine. One dinner to talk about it."

"Perfect. Let's do dinner at Weber's then. They have phenomenal steaks."

He squints at me. "At my hotel?"

"Oh, is that where you're staying? What a coinkydink."

Chapter 6

Grayson

Being back in Michigan is more nostalgic than I thought it'd be. Especially since it's the end of summer, right before fall is about to break. I love this time of year.

I should have argued with Parker about the location of our dinner. I'm trying not to think too much about the fact that I have a room with a bed six floors up from where he's meeting me.

He said six, sharp.

I anxiously glance at the clock as it ticks past six. I shouldn't be surprised. Parker is always late for everything. Guess he hasn't changed in that way.

Finally, at a quarter past, he walks through the doors. He looks like he belongs on a runway, if bulky hunks walked the runway, that is. His parents definitely taught him how to dress. Money will do that for you.

Hell, they taught me how to dress, which really came in handy when I started working at a sports talent agency in New York. Now, I can just barely afford some decent clothes with my most recent promotion.

Parker holds his arms out to me and as if under his spell I find myself standing up from the table and meeting him in a hug.

If this is any indication of the way tonight is going, I'm in big trouble.

"You look damn fine Gray," Parker whistles loudly and people turn around to frown at us, not that Parker cares. That's him in a nutshell.

"You look good, too," I find myself saying before I can stop. I didn't mean to compliment his looks. I mean he does look insanely delicious.

Of course, he breaks out in a victorious smile. Damn him.

"Nothing's going to happen tonight," I remind him.

He pouts. Why is his pout so fucking irresistible?

I raise one eyebrow at him and lower my gaze.

Finally, he relaxes back into an easy smile. "Your call, baby. You hold all the cards."

If only he knew how wrong he is about that...

I find myself getting angry that he has this power over me. *Hold it together Price.* I've rubbed elbows with the rich and famous of New York. I don't fan out over a college boy.

But he's not just any college boy, that little voice reminds me. No, he's not. He's a star goalie who easily outplayed me four years ago, and I was going pro at the time. He could have dropped out of college and signed back then. Parker's going to be a legend.

I'm in awe of the man. I take a breath to steady myself.

The waiter stops at our table and the tension breaks for a moment.

"We'll take the Stag's Head Cab," Parker orders.

I glance back at the menu and damn. "That's a three-hundred-dollar bottle of wine." I don't mean to say it aloud, but I'm shocked at his choice.

He shrugs. "Astor's paying, right?"

I nod.

"It's a good wine. Wait until you taste it."

The waiter brings back the bottle and pours a splash in a glass for Parker. He swirls and sniffs and sips in that fancy way wine enthusiasts do where they suck air over the liquid in their mouths.

Parker nods his approval and the waiter finishes pouring both our glasses.

I take a sip and he watches me. The liquid is smooth with a touch of bitterness that makes my tongue sing.

Parker smiles at my reaction. Then he orders us lobster apple salads, which sounds weird but tastes amazing.

Talking hockey with Parker is the most fun I've had in what ... years? Damn, that's sad. I don't have a lot of friends in hockey anymore. Clients, yes. Friends, no.

It's clear we both love the sport. We talk about MU and rival teams we both hate—those damn Eastern University Eagles.

We laugh about Coach Reiner and slip into some talk about his dream teams after college. Though I'm quick to point out he won't likely get picked up by any of them because he'll be drafted so early. He'll be with the worst teams, not the best.

When the check comes and I hand over the company card, I start to remember why he picked this restaurant. He wants to go upstairs with me.

"You should show me your room." He stares into my eyes, confirming my suspicions.

It's such a bad idea. I've learned I suck at casual relationships, for one. I always develop feelings for someone when I sleep with them, which ends in a lot of heartache.

Parker is young. Too young for a relationship. Probably doesn't want one. More importantly, I'm also supposed to be convincing him to sign with Astor, with me. That's a conflict of interest, perhaps against some company policy, probably could cost me my agent license.

I shake my head. "We can't."

His smile temporarily twitches. "We should have three years ago. We need a redo." He licks his lips. My pulse riots in my veins.

I swallow hard. Every fiber of my being wants to ask him upstairs.

"Just one time." He smirks. The way his words ring in my ears makes me float. I shouldn't be floating.

Before I can process how to stop this, I'm grabbing his hand and pulling him toward the elevators.

Chapter 7

Parker

Grayson is holding my hand and dragging me back to his cave to fuck my brains out. Or maybe I'll fuck his brains out. Either way, there will be brain matter to clean off the walls and floor and ceiling when I'm done with him. I'll need to leave a big tip for the cleaning staff before I go.

I want to maul him in the elevator, but someone gets on with us. I'm goddamn giddy with anticipation. When we step out and bound down to his room, I press my dick into his ass while he runs the key card through the door.

He makes a little sound in the back of his throat. *Fucking hell!*

I close the door behind me as I kick off my shoes and peel off my shirt. My cock is already heavy and begging for him.

"Whoa ..." Grayson turns to look at me. "You work fast."

"I don't want you to change your mind." I unbuckle my belt.

"And being naked will solidify your case?"

I pull off my pants so that I'm down to my jock style undies. "You tell me." I spin around to show him the open back.

He lets out a slow dramatic breath that leaves me with a smirk on my lips. He tugs at the thick bulge in his pants.

"So that's a yes," I growl at him.

"Come here," he commands. If he's taking charge, I'm game.

I walk over obediently.

He brushes his thumb on my bottom lip, pulling it down slightly.

I want him to touch me everywhere, lick me everywhere. I'm eager for it. His restraint is torture.

With his thumb still on my lip, he kisses the corners of my mouth in succession. His kisses are gentle and slow and cause me to breathe out a sigh of relief. I feel my eagerness calming a little.

He looks right at me and shakes his head. "Don't rush it. If we're going to make a colossal mistake, let's do it right."

I nod with a dumbfounded expression on my face. He's right though. We should make this last. I don't know when it could happen again. He lives in New York; I have a year of school left. Who knows where I'll be signed after I graduate.

"Can I at least take off your shirt?" I ask as I gasp for air, trying my best to keep my neediness under control.

"Yes, you may." He smirks. I grab at the hem and start to pull it off, but he grabs my wrists. "Sloooowly."

I whine a little, but I do as he says, and very slowly peel off his shirt. *Argh!*

I give him my puppy eyes in question. *What can I do next?* I want to scream and jump around.

He grabs my face, and places our lips together. The softness calms me a touch more.

I breathe in and out through my nose, inhaling the scent of him which is mixed with thick wine. It's heavenly.

Finally, he pushes past my lips. My tongue meets his and I want to go wild licking at him, but I hold myself back by some miracle. We tilt our heads to get a deeper angle as we glide over each other. My eyes close and I savor him like he's my last meal. I forgot how good just kissing him is.

My hands reach up automatically to grab him and pull him close, so our bodies are pressing together. I need some kind of friction before I bounce off the goddamn walls.

He doesn't stop me as I start pressing my package onto him with small, controlled thrusts.

In fact, I feel him matching me, so we rock harder into one another. I run one hand up the back of his neck into the shaved part of his hair, cupping him in my palm.

I revel in the heat of his body, the softness of our skin contrasted with the hardness of our muscles. He feels so right, as if we are puzzle pieces made to fit. I don't know that I've ever had that before. This moment is perfection.

His hands trail down to his pants, unfastening them with a flick of his fingers. To my surprise, even as I calm down and start to enjoy the pace, he's getting more frantic. His jeans drop to the floor. My fingers tickle a trail down his back to reach his ass. The thin swatch of fabric is all that's left. I want it gone too.

Our cocks are perfectly aligned, I grind them together, swollen and straining for freedom. I feel his fingers pressing under the straps on my underwear, peeling them down and off. They swish to the floor. I copy him and take his down, too. Finally, we are touching our full lengths, veiny and throbbing and leaking.

"I need you, now," Grayson rasps to my surprise.

I jump at his words, reaching back for the wallet in my jeans pocket to grab the supplies.

"Which way?" I ask as I drop my jeans back into a crumbled pile on the floor.

"Top me." His words suck the air from my lungs. Fuck. Yes. Please.

I wrap myself up immediately as I kiss him again. I want every inch of him on my tongue, on my dick. I walk us back toward the bed and shove him down. I crawl up over him as he backs his way up to the headboard. When he goes too far up, I pull him by the legs until he's in the middle of the bed splayed out for me.

I drop onto the side of him and he hikes a leg up, I lean down and take his dick into my mouth. He no longer tells me to go slow. I push him as far back in my throat as I can and suck and lap him as I work my slicked finger into his crack and press inside him. He accepts me easily and I add a second finger. I can't wait to press my dick inside his hot channel. I want to be pushy, but I try my best to be patient.

When he moans, "I'm ready," in between breaths, I almost lose it. I should have taken care of myself before I got here. I won't be lasting very long, but damn it I will try my hardest.

I don't waste a beat before I sheath up and I climb on top of him and kiss him deeply as I reach between us and line up my crown with his tight muscle. I slowly push into him and he groans into my mouth. I pause to let him adjust, but he grabs my hips and pulls me in until my balls touch his ass. The feeling is downright spiritual.

I break our kiss because I need to watch his face. I don't think I've ever needed to do that before. But this time, I do. I need to see each muscle twitch, each breath he sucks in, I need to watch the way his mouth moves when he moans.

I start slowly, as much for him as for me, but that doesn't last long. I can't help myself. In minutes I'm rocking into him as hard as I can, dragging out to my tip and then slamming hard back in again.

His mouth drops open on a thrust and I know I hit his sweet spot. I hold myself inside him and peg it over and over again. He moans loudly on each breath, timed with each thrust. Every glorious muscle in his body is tensed. I feel him clamp down on my dick as he starts to throb and erupt in thick ribbons that coat his chest.

The sight has me filling the condom in seconds. I have just enough energy to fall onto him and kiss his mouth before I'm lost to the post-sex haze.

Drunk on Grayson Price for the second time in my life, now I know there's no way I'll let this be the last time. I bet my career on it.

Chapter 8

Grayson

I didn't mean for it to happen, but after Parker came, there was no moving him. I managed to roll him off me. I peeled off the condom carefully and washed us up. He grunted as I worked around him. When I laid back down, he scooped me up so tight I couldn't move. It felt damn good laying there in his arms and I easily fell asleep.

He insisted he drive me to the airport the next day. It was hard to say goodbye. After he kissed me at the airport, I refused to eat or drink on the plane. I wanted to savor every drop of him. I should definitely not have let that all go down. But it was pretty fucking worth it.

As I arrive to work the next day, my boss is pacing outside my office door.

"So, how was Parker?" John asks with wide eyes.

I choke on my coffee because his words carry a different meaning for me now. I have no idea what to tell him, but he's waiting for an answer. "He's interested." I don't know if that's a fair assessment, but the words are out there now.

I feel sick in my gut as I debate Parker's words. He'll consider Astor, but only with me. And yet he sunk himself deep inside me and rocked my goddam world off its axis. I'm so royally fucked now. Not only am I crushing on an unattainable man, but my company wants this account more than any other in the country.

Parker's going to bring in tens of millions. We already have sponsors sending in early offers and the guy isn't signed to us yet, let alone drafted to an NHL team. It's madness.

Parker's name has been on the company's lips since the first day I started with them, but as he made clear, he wasn't making any deals until graduation. So, naturally, his senior year has sent all the sharks swimming as if there's blood in the water.

John rambles on about Parker and how important he is to our future and yells at me to close the deal. Great. I slink down to my work wife Sadie's office and close her door.

"Hey girl," I plunk down in her spare chair.

She peers over her monitor at me. "What's wrong, Gray?"

"In theory, what would happen if I became romantically involved with a client?"

She pushes off her desk and rolls her chair over to me. "In theory?" she questions, one eyebrow cocked.

I nod.

She closes her eyes and pinches the bridge of her nose. "You'd be fucked."

I sink at her words. "That bad, huh?"

"Astor is strict. Other agencies have different rules. But yeah. Here that's like a number one no-no."

"Shit." My stomach is tying into knots.

"You didn't fuck a client, did you?"

"Only a prospective one," I admit. I probably shouldn't, but I trust Sadie with my life. She's the person who got me through the mess I called life when I first got to New York.

"Babe, you need to end that shit ASAP. I'd hand them off, too. Make something up. You've been on fire here, don't end in flames."

"You're right. Hey, can you take him?" I feign a smile.

"Who is it?"

"Parker Miller."

"Fuck, he's insanely hot! Your friend Sadie wants to high five you about that one. But yeah, laugh it up bitch. They'd never give me a client like Parker. How'd you even get him?"

"We had a friend connection, they thought it'd give us an edge for signing. The shitty part is, Parker said he'd only consider us if I am his agent."

Sadie goes back to pinching the bridge of her nose. "You are soooo messy, Gray."

Chapter 9

Parker

It's always weird moving back into the Sigma frat house at the end of the summer. Some people stick around all year. I usually attend hockey training camp and stay at home for a few weeks.

Now I'm in the senior wing of the house with Johnny Xu and Chase Henry. They've been my best friends since we were little. We've played hockey together forever. We still play together.

Chase is good enough to take it somewhere if he wants, but I get the feeling he's over it. Johnny is awesome as a college defenseman, but that's probably where his journey ends.

When the semester starts, I remember why I love college so much. Our house throws awesome parties and our kickoff party is no exception. It's our annual ABC party— Anything But Clothes.

Last year we made what I called man-skirts out of cereal boxes. Captain Crunch to be precise, although Johnny used Count Chocula and Chase used Boo Berry boxes.

This year we've got a bunch of feather boas that we're fashioning into some semblance of clothing, sans tops. Chase and Johnny are good sports, always going along with my wild ideas since we were kids.

Our frat is also known as the queerest frat on campus, so no one gets homophobic when three guys show up in matching feather boas. If they did, the other brothers would drag them out by their ankles.

"Xu, snap a pic of me!" I toss him my phone. I put my hands on my hips and pose like I'm a superhero, making sure to flex all my muscles. I promptly send the photo to Grayson.

Parker: *You like my creation???*

Grayson: …

Parker: *When you coming back to woo me?*

Grayson: *SMH. You are trouble.*

Parker: *Video chat later? *cue innocent smile on my face**

Grayson: *OK*

I'm sure I'm grinning like a goof right now.

"Who are you texting that to?" Chase raises his eyebrow at me.

"Grayson Price." I smile widely.

"Is this for official Astor recruiting or are you trying to recruit Grayson onto your dick again?" Xu laughs.

"Both, for sure," I brag. I tell my friends everything and hookups are no exception.

They didn't approve of my plan to not have Grayson tell his agency about what we did, but they said they understood.

"You're so in love with him." Chase shakes his head at me.

I shrug. "Boyhood crushes on older men, am I right?"

They both look at me in confusion. Xu is straight, as far as we know. Chase doesn't seem to have crushes.

I guess it's just me, then.

All the brothers gather in the living room as we open the doors and cue the music. We usually have a line around the house, but tonight it's even longer.

The newest pledges will work the doors as bouncers, turning away anyone in clothes and people without a student ID.

The costumes so far are hilarious. Luca, who is also bisexual, is wearing a twister game board.

Yup. These are the antics I'm going to miss most.

As usual, I'm totally swarmed by puck bunnies and puck bucks. Yeah, that's right. Puck bucks— aka male rabbits— because I need a way to brag about the horny male hockey fans who swoon over handsome queer hockey players like myself. Give me time to hit the NHL and I swear it will catch on.

When my phone vibrates, I know it's Grayson. I want to video chat with him, so I have no trouble leaving the groupies behind. I've been trying to get a hold of him for a few weeks. He said he was busy, though.

I'm shocked he even agreed to a call tonight.

I close my bedroom door and dial him. His face pops on my screen. What a gorgeous sight.

"Hey you!" I beam while holding my phone out, angling it so he can see my bare chest.

"You are evil," he accuses me.

"It seems to work for you." I wink at him.

He shakes his head. "We should talk, Park." He sounds serious.

I don't let it shake me though. "Talk away, baby," I sing.

He rubs his hands on his temple. "It turns out Astor is, like, very anti fucking-your-potential-clients and very pro me-trying-to-sign-you. So, I'm in a pickle here."

I want to make a joke about the pickle thing, but I manage to hold back because Gray seems genuinely stressed. "Babe, this is an easy fix."

"It is?" He perks up.

"For sure. Just quit."

"Quit my job because we fucked once? Okay, you so don't get how adulting works." He shakes his head in quiet exasperation.

"Start your own agency. I'll be your first client. Then we can fuck more. I'm horny. See?" I angle the phone down and lift my feather boa to reveal my hard on.

"Fuck, Parker," he scolds me. "Put that thing away."

I turn the camera back to my face. "Think about it. It's a good idea."

"It's a terrible idea for numerous reasons." He scoffs.

"Name one," I challenge.

"You could get injured like I did. You shouldn't make career decisions based on one night of great sex. You won't be making money for any agent until at least ten months from now. That's three solid reasons." He looks smug, like he's bested me.

"All I heard was the part about great sex. We should do that again. Get on a plane. I'll send you a ticket." I wink.

He groans in frustration. "I'm so getting fired."

"You make it sound like I'm not worth it!" I claim offense, clutching my hand to my chest. "Did I not show you …" I flash my dick on the camera again.

"This is why I don't call, for the record."

"You love it and you know it. Come on. Let's do a little MM."

"MM?"

"Mutual masturbation," I explain. "I already started."

He gasps. "Fucking hell, Park. You are bossy."

"You like it, and you're hard."

"You can't see my dick," he argues.

"But you are, aren't you?" I say confidently as he gives me a pointed look. "Show me." I up nod at him.

He bites his full bottom lip and then angles the camera down. He's in pajama pants that are, indeed, heavily tented.

"Wrap your fingers around that fat cock of yours. Pretend it's my hand," I command.

He keeps the camera on his face, but he nods, and I see his arm moving.

"Good. Now stroke it real slow but squeeze it hard." I watch his face while he does it. His eyes are clenched shut. God damn that's hot. I rip off my feather boa contraption and lay on my bed, setting my phone up on a pillow so my naked body is in the camera.

"Look at me while you do it," I tell him.

He opens his eyes and groans.

I take my dick in my hand. "Follow my lead," I instruct. I rub my thumb over the tip and work the pre-cum over it.

"Yeessss," he groans.

"Go faster. Do it like you're balls deep inside me, about to fill my ass with your cum."

"Fuck Parker …" he starts to say but his brows clench together. He cries out and I know he's there.

I race after him, watching him, wishing he was inside me. I let myself shoot haphazardly on my bed, some hits the floor, some lands on my thighs. "Damn, Gray bae. I loved that."

"Gray bae?" he asks.

"Yup." I wink.

"Your body is ri-donk-ulous." He changes the subject.

"I'm sending you a ticket for this weekend. I need more wooing."

"Not happening."

"See you at the airport, bae," I tell him as I end our call.

Chapter 10

Grayson

I can't believe I got on this plane. Parker is a bad influence on me. My self-control is apparently shit, as far as he's concerned. And why the fuck did my heart leap when he called me bae?

I clearly need a doctor. I must have some sort of vitamin deficiency that's causing me to make shit decisions. Either that, or I must be self-destructive because I'm risking my career for what—a fling with a hot guy?

He's not just any hot guy, though. He's Parker—silly, gorgeous, lights up a room, makes me come oh-so-good.

God, Cameron would kill me if he found out. Which he won't. This is just a one-time fling. This will be my last time.

Just to be sure, before I leave, I tell my boss at Astor that Parker doesn't want to work with me. I say Parker's asked for a more experienced agent. That's a very reasonable lie. Because Parker is so high profile, he can do that kind of thing.

John buys it without question. He reassigns the job to Kendrick Stone, our top agent.

I'm sure I'm still forbidden from messing around with Parker despite that, but I feel a little relief already.

Parker would have been a career changing client, but I could never take advantage of him like that.

Standing outside with the other arrivals at the airport, I spot him in his dark SUV, even through the tinted windows. I can just see a glimpse of his backward hat. A-fucking-dorable.

I hop in the passenger seat.

"Hey, bae." He leans over and kisses me. "I'm glad you're home."

"You're very manipulative," I accuse him as he pulls away from the pickup lane.

He shrugs at my charge. "True."

"I can't believe you were on time to get me."

He laughs. "I had incentive for this."

"Sex?" I chuckle.

"Seeing you. But yeah, sex is a good motivator, too."

"So I need to tell you something right off the bat," I start.

"That Astor has a new agent assigned to work me over?"

"Well, yeah." I'm surprised Kendrick moved that fast. Then again, I should have expected it. "Our relationship is too confusing already. I'd never know if you were signing with me for me, or because you were really horny at the time."

"It would have been both, for the record. I don't trust anyone more than I trust you, Gray. And I am reeeaaaallly horny." He grabs my hand and places it on his hard cock over his rather thin sweatpants.

"Well at least I'm not a sleezy agent now. We can have our hat-trick fuck."

"Ha! Yes, I like that. But there is a problem with your logic."

"What's that?"

"We've definitely fucking more than three times this weekend. A lot more. We'll be flying back and forth for the foreseeable future."

"That sounds like an expensive way to get laid, Park," I protest.

"Psh. You're not just a fuck. I've wanted you for as long as I've wanted cock in my mouth. I feel like I'm finally in your league," Parker tells me.

"Finally in *my* league? I think you have that backwards."

Parker reaches over the console and holds my hand, to my surprise.

"But for real, if you want Astor, you can have them now. No strings."

"I want to work with you. When you wisen up and start your own agency, we'll be golden."

"That's a terrible idea. I don't have the resources or connections."

"We'll make them together."

He does have a point. No matter who he signs with, opportunities are going to knock down his door. Although that little nagging thought in my mind is still there—if what happened to me happens to him. *He's not you Grayson.* It's true. My doctors told me that my injury was rare. Odds are Parker will have a long healthy career.

When we arrive at the frat house, I feel like I'm back in college again. I mean, I'm only twenty-four, but it's still weird to be back in this world. I grab my bag and follow Parker to his room. In minutes, we're naked and kissing frantically.

"I want you inside me," Parker rasps.

My eyes pop wide open and my heart hammers at his words. My mouth goes dry. He senses my hesitation and his brow snaps together. "What's wrong?"

"I've never done that," I admit.

"Really? Power bottom? Huh. Never would have pegged you for that. Pun intended."

I shake my head at his bad joke, but I can't help smiling a little. "I'm not a power bottom, it's just that I've never really wanted to top before."

"And do you still not want to?"

I purse my lips together. "If I'm being honest, not really. It's nothing personal."

"You don't have to explain, Gray. We'll do whatever you want. Besides, I love fucking you. Let's definitely do lots of that."

"Thank you."

"But maybe just a finger in me?" he asks as he gives me his adorable puppy dog eyes and I laugh.

"Maybe."

"Maybe just a lick of my hole?"

I snort laugh. "Yeah no. That's terrifying."

"Why is my butthole suddenly the holy grail?" He gives me a wicked smile.

"Because when someone tells you no, you have to have that thing ten times more?"

"You are not wrong sweet cheeks," Parker agrees while he slaps my ass.

"Enough taunting me," I say as I stroke my dick lazily. "Come fuck me into this mattress."

"Yes sir!" Parker pushes my legs apart and crawls between them without another word.

Chapter 11

Parker

"I need to be the mature one here." Grayson's words cut through me like a hot knife into cold butter.

I knew something was wrong this morning. He was acting very distant and he wouldn't even go another round with me. Maybe that's for the best because I'm sure his ass is sore.

"You're no fun," I complain.

"Adulting is no fun. Well, at least for most of us. You'll be a famous celebrity soon. Adulting for you will essentially be trying to stay out of trouble."

"That's why I need you!" I protest.

"It's not happening. Sign with Kendrick if you want Astor. He'll be great."

"Is that boyfriend Grayson's advice or agent Grayson's advice?" I ask.

Grayson rubs his hand through his hair. "We're not boyfriends, Park. We had some fun this weekend, but it needs to end here. I live in a different state. I'm in a very different place in life. You have a big career starting soon. Can we just leave it at fun?"

Everything he's saying to me right now hurts. I have no idea why he's back peddling after such an awesome weekend.

I clench my jaw as hard as I can as he opens the door of the SUV.

"I gotta go. I have a plane to catch," he reminds me as he steps out, not even kissing me goodbye.

My heart aches instantly.

I feel tears threatening to spill over as I watch him walk away through the big glass doors. He doesn't even look back at me. I can't help but feel used and confused.

I peel away from the curb dramatically and call Chase to complain. When he doesn't answer I call Johnny. When he doesn't answer I turn the radio up all the way and drown out my thoughts.

By the time I pull into the driveway of the frat house, I see I have a few missed texts from Grayson.

Grayson: *I'm sorry if I made you feel bad. I'm having a hard time resisting you TBH, but we're on different planets right now.*

Grayson: *Please don't hate me.*

Different planets? That's stupid. I'm getting sick of this whole him seeing me only as a kid thing.

I'm an adult, sort of. But I know what I want. I've always been that way. Very sure of myself. Sure of what I need and what I want. I can't stand to write him back.

I open a message to my brother instead. It's petty, but I don't care.

Parker: *Talk some sense into your idiot BFF.*

Cameron: *What are you talking about?*

Parker: *He won't be my boyfriend. How stupid is that?*

My phone rings a second later. Maybe I should have waited for Chase or Johnny to be free to talk after all. Damn, I am impulsive.

"Yello," I answer with fake calmness.

"What the fuck Park? What happened?"

"I like Grayson. Be a good big brother and make him date me," I beg.

"Where is this even coming from?" Cameron's clearly confused.

I don't want to fully betray Grayson, even more than I just have. "We've been talking because Astor wants me to sign with them and now, I have a full-on crush on him."

"More so than you have over the last seven years?" he asks.

"Oh, you knew about that?" My face reddens but luckily, he can't see that.

"Dude, you're so obvious. You followed him around like a lost puppy."

"Oh. Well, now I want to be his boyfriend," I state matter-of-factly.

"He lives in another state and his agency wants to sign you. I don't think it's in the cards little bro."

"Fuck the cards, Cam. He should start his own agency and sign me. Then he can live wherever I live and …"

Cameron cuts me off. "Hold up. Now you want to live with him? Jesus, Park, you're twenty-one, that's way too young to talk like that."

"I don't care how old I am. Grayson is everything, man. Everything. I want him to take me seriously. Please help me." I'm not even ashamed of how obvious I'm being. My heart's right on my sleeve here. I'm desperate.

Cameron sighs. "Grayson's had a hard life. It seems like he's finally doing well, now. If you actually do care about him, leave him alone. It'd be a risk for him to start an agency by himself. He needs stability. Just let it go."

"Well fuck." I click off my seat belt, slam my door, and march to my room.

"You can say that again. I'm still pissed, too, you know. Liking Grayson is a major bro code violation."

"Okay, well thanks for all the help," I say, my tone drenched in sarcasm.

"Sorry brother."

I click to hang up without another word. This is such bullshit because I know it in my goddam gut that Grayson and I are supposed to be together. Nothing has ever made more sense to me.

***

"It's time to come out of your room. I don't know what's got you in a funk, but the holiday party is starting, we need you to rally." My mom is doing her best to cheer me up. "Seriously Park, I've never seen you like this. You're scaring me."

"I have a crush who doesn't like me back," I whine.

Her face is pure shock for a moment until it bleeds into her intrigued expression. "That's a first for you, isn't it?"

I nod.

"Well, love has highs and lows. It's a rollercoaster ride. Sometimes, it works out and then it doesn't. I know that's a little blunt, but I'm just saying that you're young and there are more people to meet out there. So, come down and enjoy the party. Flirt a little, drink a little, it will take your mind off things."

I'm so sick of being called young, but I don't snap at my mom. "That's some solid parenting right there, Mom."

She laughs. "You know me, Park. I'm all real, all the time. Hey, you know who's going to be here? Dr. Goldberg's son, Micah. He just came out."

"Are you wingmanning me?"

"Is that not what moms do?"

"I don't know. I kinda like it." I follow my mom downstairs to our annual holiday party.

She introduces me to Micah. He is admittedly hot, but I feel nothing for him. I want Grayson.

I fake my way through the conversation. Usually chatting comes easy to me. I'm a social butterfly after all. Not in this moment, though. I'm pretty sure I'm scowling at him. I can tell he's looking for a way out.

"I don't know why they always think two gay guys want to meet each other," he says dryly.

"I'm bi actually, but I hear you."

"Oh, you're one of those?"

"Don't hate." My frown deepens.

"Everything okay over here?" My heart leaps at the voice. It's Grayson's.

I spin around and my face lights up. I throw my arms around his neck.

Micah shuffles away at some point, I don't even see it, though. I'm over the moon that Grayson is here in front of me.

"Can I kiss you?" I ask a split second before my lips crash into his.

He kisses me back while laughing. "Yes," he says as we break away.

"Grayson?" My mom rounds the corner. She looks back and forth between us.

Grayson drops his hands from my waist and goes to hug her. "It's great to see you, Ellen. Thank you for making me come tonight."

Mom kisses his cheeks. "You've missed too many of these." She stands staring at us, hands on her hips. "So, which one of you is going to tell me what's going on? Or is it none of my business?"

"The latter, Ma," I interject.

"I'm dating your son," Grayson answers at the same time.

"Wait, what?" my mom and I say in unison and then look at each other.

She shakes her head. "Which son?"

"Well, hopefully Parker, if he'll forgive me."

"I forgive you," I say automatically.

"I'm sorry I ghosted you. That wasn't cool of me. I was scared."

"This feels like a private moment. Why don't you take Gray up to his room?" Mom suggests.

I grab his hand in mine and we head upstairs. As soon as the door is shut, I tackle him to the bed. We're instantly devouring each other's mouths, grinding our already hard cocks together.

"Fuck, I've missed you," I say between kisses. My heart is in my throat, practically choking me with joy.

"You really forgive me?" he asks.

I pause and look at him. "I'm pretty sure I'd put up with almost anything to be with you, Gray."

"Well that sounds unhealthy, but I appreciate the sentiment."

I laugh and push myself into him to remind him my dick needs attention. "As long as you've finally figured out that we belong together, everything else is just detail," I explain.

The smile on Grayson's face lifts a weight off me that I didn't even realize was there.

I feel like I can relax for the first time in weeks. "Oh, minor detail though, you have to talk to Cameron. He's pretty pissed at me about you."

Grayson scrunches his nose. "Yeah. He, um, called me. He's the reason I'm here."

I sit bolt upright. "Wait, what?"

Grayson shifts up and nods. "For real. When I told him what was bothering me and how I felt about you, he told me I was being an idiot."

"My brother? Cameron Miller?"

"The very same one," he assures me.

"What did you say about me? I feel like he knows more than I do at this point."

There's a knock at the door before he can explain. It's Cameron. "So, you guys are good then?" he asks.

I jump up and hug Cameron. "Apology accepted." I beam.

His brows furrow.

"You were a dick to me about Grayson," I accuse him.

"My bad. But hey, did I not come through?"

"Fair point. I owe you my first NHL paycheck." I grin.

"Well actually, about that...did Gray tell you our news?"

"What news?" I look back and forth between them.

"We're going in together on our own sports agency. He'll handle talent, I'll do the legal stuff."

My face lights up. "No shit! That's awesome." I hit Cameron's back before heading to hug Grayson.

"But we're not signing you," Grayson clarifies.

"Like hell you aren't," I protest.

"Yeah, what he said," Cameron agrees.

"It's a conflict of interest," Grayson argues.

I shake my head. "We're family and we're all going to bring what we have to the table on this thing. We'll be equal partners."

"Hold up." Cameron scoffs.

"That's actually brilliant. A third each. Admit it Cam, Parker's going to give us instant street cred," Grayson urges.

Cameron rolls his eyes. "Fine."

"Awesome. Now Cameron, go away because I haven't seen Grayson in weeks and I need him naked immediately."

"Aww man, I didn't need to hear that shit. New business rule, no telling me when you're banging,"

Cameron lectures us as he walks from the room and closes the door.

Chapter 12

Grayson

I hold Parker's hand. It's sweaty, as if his leg bouncing up and down isn't enough to tell me he's nervous. I give him a gentle smile and we take a breath in synchro.

Cameron sits on the other side of Parker, ringing his hands together. Dale and Ellen are next to Cameron.

Coach Reiner is two rows back with Johnny Xu and Chase Henry, who Parker insisted on inviting.

The auditorium is packed with people. This whole night is surreal.

I can't help but imagine what it might have been like four years ago if it had been me in Parker's place. I'm happy to live vicariously through him, though. Honestly.

He comes off as cocky, but he's humble and grateful and overall amazing. Damn, I love my man. Being with him and feeling right in the world makes me happy that I fucked up my groin, because if I hadn't, I would have been off traveling the country playing hockey. Still in the closet and completely missing out on the love of my life. This way is definitely better.

The lights drop low and music plays. The audience quiets as a woman takes the stage and welcomes us to the Arena for the NHL draft. The room is electric. Parker pulls my hand up to his lips and kisses the back of it. I wink at him.

I don't expect Parker will have to wait long. He's a shoo-in for first round picks. I won't be surprised if he's one of the first two picks, he's really that good.

The first team up is Ottawa. They have a stellar goalie and we're not expecting them to take Parker. They don't. Instead they take a young center out of the juniors. Next is Los Angeles. They may take Parker. We all hold our breath as the head Coach takes the stage.

"In the second pick, Los Angeles is proud to select, from Michigan University, goal tender Parker Miller!" The crowd erupts in applause and we all shoot out of our seats at his name and hug him in succession.

As Parker wedges his way out from the tight aisle, Johnny and Chase meet him for a hug. Then his old coach shakes his hand before an usher comes and escorts Parker to the stage.

Parker shimmy's out of his suit coat and hands it off to someone as he takes the stage. The team's administration waits in a long line. Each of them takes a turn shaking his hand and hugging him. I can see words exchanged and smiles all around.

Someone passes him a hat and a jersey. He pulls the jersey over his head and he spins to show off the big "Miller" on the back, pointing at it with two thumbs over his shoulders. The crowd goes wild. Then he places the team's cap on his head.

I've seen this a dozen times on TV, but this hits so different now that it's my man on stage.

I'm acutely aware that someone hands me Parker's suit coat. I fold it in my lap as I watch Parker wrap arms around his new team leadership and pose for a picture. They sweep him off the stage and interview him. His face lights up the Megatron.

"How do you feel being the second pick of the first round?" the interviewer asks.

"I'm ecstatic to be a part of L.A. They are a great team and I can't wait to hit the ice with them." Parker flashes his winning smile as they cut to a video of the L.A. fans at the watch party jumping up and down for him. I'm shook. This is the real deal isn't it? It's insane.

The Megatron flashes replays of him putting his jersey on and hugging his mom. Pictures from his younger days play in a slideshow. A cameraman and reporter come to our aisle and ask Ellen questions about Parker.

Finally, the vice president for L.A. takes an interview and talks about how lucky they are to have a player like Parker. "We've been watching him a long time and we're excited about what he can bring to this team and to this league."

Damn. I think I have to wipe a tear from my eye. I am so proud of Parker in this moment, I could literally burst.

Chapter 13

Parker

Tonight was insanely magical.

I am officially an NHL player. I'm moving to L.A. and Grayson is coming with me.

It's an agonizing three hours of draft picks until I can get out of here and celebrate properly. My parents insist on taking us out, even though I am eager to get back to my hotel room so Grayson can ride my dick like I'm a damn pony, you know, romantic style.

Finally the party dies down and we make our excuses and head to bed.

Grayson looks at me so intently, my heart melts.

"What?" I ask.

"You are something else, Parker Miller."

"So are you." I undo my tie.

Grayson grabs it before I can and tugs me to the bed, right down on top of him. "Parker, I love you."

I smile. He's said it before, but I never get tired of hearing it. "I love you, too, Grayson Price."

"I'm so proud of you."

"Psh. You're the amazing one. You started an entire agency and signed three athletes in six months. I want to ask you something." I stand up from the bed and he sits down on it.

"Okay," he agrees cautiously.

I nip at his lips and pin his arms back. "Will you be my husband?" I ask.

His eyes go wide. "Are you serious?"

"Very," I confirm. "And please don't with that 'you're too young, you're not gay' bit."

He laughs at my call back to when he protested kissing me all those years ago.

"Okay," he states plainly with a big smile on his face.

"Okay?" I clarify as my smile breaks out onto my already sore cheeks.

He nods. "You are like a beam of sunshine, Parker. You light everything up. You feel like home to me, no matter where we are. There was a time when I envied you because you had what I wanted, but even then, I still admired you. You are humble and kind. Being with you makes every second of life better. You really know how to have fun. I want that with you. All of it. So yes. I'll be your husband."

"Wow, that was a better proposal than mine." I lean down and kiss his soft lips.

"It's not a competition." His voice is low.

"Never. Not with you. You win. That's all there is to it," I concede.

"What happened to the Parker Miller who always gets what he wants?"

"Well, I got you, now. The rest is irrelevant detail."

"Even the NHL?"

"Well, maybe not the NHL," I agree, and we laugh before we return to peeling off each other's clothes.

"There's something I've been waiting to tell you ..." Grayson pauses and looks serious.

"What's that?" I ask as a look of concern crosses my face.

"I'm ready," he says and I instantly know what he means.

"Fucking hell. This really is the best night of my life."

Grayson gives me a booming laugh that I love.

"Just be gentle with me. I haven't bottomed in a while," I plead.

"Always baby. Always."

Up next in the series is a steamy read you do *not* want to miss! *Nice Guys Finish First* is about a shy hockey player and bad boy... Chase is just figuring out his sexuality and Luca is all too happy to show him a new version of *stick handling*. The high-steam first times will clear your pores, full facial style. IT. IS. SO. ON.

Want More Spicy Sweetness?

Other Books by Billie Bloom

The Bromance Chronicles
Trouble On Top
Nice Guys Finish First
Out With A Bang
Pucked Up Love

Stand Alone Novels
Blow Me Away

Thank you!

Thanks for checking out my debut MM romance novella! I am honored you gave it a read and I can't wait to share the rest of the series with you. A huge thanks goes out to Kendall Ryan for being my guide and beta reader. Thank you to the wonderful K.C. Enders for the phenomenal proofing and editing. And thank you, the beautiful queer romance community for being so welcoming. You are amazing! xoxo

Let's Stay in Touch Baddies!

Visit billiebloomromance.com to join my reader list.

Find me on Facebook and join my group, Billie's Baddies.

You can also find me on Goodreads, TikTok, Bookbub, Twitter, and Instagram. Whew.

About the Author

Billie Bloom lives in the state where people think fifty degrees is shorts weather and they point to where they're from using their hand as a map. They swoon for steamy queer romance that makes their mouth drop open like a fish, and their spouse ask curiously, *what are you doing over there?* As a lover of the genre, they can often be found in a trance-like state drooling out of one side of their mouth as they write (or read) up to sixteen hours a day – you know, as one does. Billie is shamelessly obsessed with fictitious frat bros, alpha jocks, and most *especially,* sassy twinks.

Made in United States
Orlando, FL
06 December 2022